Bible Stories

Miles Kelly

First published in 2017 by Miles Kelly Publishing Ltd
Harding's Barn, Bardfield End Green, Thaxted, Essex, CM6 3PX, UK

Copyright © Miles Kelly Publishing Ltd 2017
This edition printed 2021

2 4 6 8 10 9 7 5 3 1

Publishing Director Belinda Gallagher
Creative Director Jo Cowan
Editorial Director Rosie Neave
Senior Editors Fran Bromage, Becky Miles
Design Managers Joe Jones, Simon Lee
Image Manager Liberty Newton
Production Jennifer Brunwin
Reprographics Stephan Davis
Assets Lorraine King

ISBN 978-1-78989-301-4

Printed in China

British Library Cataloguing-in-Publication Data
A catalogue record for this book is available from the British Library

ACKNOWLEDGEMENTS
The publishers would like to thank the following artists who have contributed to this book:
Noah and the Ark: Anna Jones (The Bright Agency)
Joseph and his Coat of Many Colours: Laura Watson (Advocate Art)
Moses in the Bulrushes: Kay Widdowson (Advocate Art)
David and Goliath: Nacho Gomez (Advocate Art)

Made with paper from a sustainable forest

www.mileskelly.net

Noah and the Ark

When God first made the world,
it was very beautiful.
Everything was peaceful and
everyone was happy.

But people did not **respect** **the world** or each other.

This made God **sad.**

5

People were selfish, cruel and wicked.
They were mean to each other, and
fought over everything.
This made God angry.

One man above all others was
good, **honest** and hard-working.

His name was Noah.
God **was pleased** with Noah, his wife
and their three sons and wives.

So, one night God spoke
to Noah in a **dream.**

"I am going to flood the
world and **wash it clean**
again," God told Noah.

"You will need to build a **huge wooden ark** to save your family and two of every living creature."

The next day, Noah, his wife, their sons and their wives began the **enormous task** God had given them.

They used the best wood they could find and **slowly** the ark took shape.

"We must give it a roof of reeds and **coat it with tar** to make it water-tight," said Noah.

11

Next, Noah collected one pair of **every animal**, just as God had asked him to.

12

The animals walked, hopped, crawled, slithered and were carried **two by two** onto the ark.

Noah's neighbours laughed at him, but Noah **trusted God.**

13

One week later, God sent the first storm clouds and it **began to rain.**

Rivers, lakes and oceans quickly swelled. Water flooded the land and the ark **floated away.**

But Noah and his family
trusted God to
keep them safe.

15

It rained and it rained, and the world was **washed clean** by an enormous flood, as God had wished.

16

Soon even the **highest mountains** were covered by the water, and still the rain came.

It rained for **forty days and forty nights,** then as quickly as it started, it stopped.

The ark came to rest on
the top of a **huge mountain.**
"I can't see anything but water,"
said Noah, peeking out.

Then God sent a **wind** to begin drying up the water and the **sun** shone down on the flood.

19

Noah waited for a week, then he sent out a **raven**.

"If there is **dry land** anywhere, the raven will find it," he said to himself.

But the raven soon came back to the ark.
Noah **waited another week**
and then sent out a dove.

This time the **dove** flew
back with an olive branch.

When Noah **sent the dove out** the next week, it did not return. The dove had found land.

God said to Noah: "The flood is over. It is time for you and your family to leave the ark."

"Go out into the world with the creatures and **begin again,**" said God.

23

God promised never to flood the world again. As a sign of His vow, He made a **rainbow**...

...to remind everyone of **His promise.**

24

Joseph
and his Coat
of Many Colours

There once was a man called Jacob who had twelve sons.

His favourite sons were Joseph and 26 Benjamin, but he **loved** Joseph the most.

When Joseph turned seventeen, Jacob gave him a beautiful coat of many different colours.

This made Joseph's brothers very jealous. 27

One night, Joseph had
a strange dream.
He told his brothers
about it the next day.

"I dreamt that we were in the fields
at harvest time and all of your bundles
of wheat bowed down to mine."

28

Then Joseph dreamt
that the sun, moon and
eleven stars bowed to him.

When Joseph told his brothers
about the dream they became very angry.
"You think we will bow down to you?"

29

One day, Joseph went to look for his brothers while they were out **working**.

When the brothers saw Joseph approaching in his beautiful coat, they **plotted** against him.

"I wish we could get rid
of him once and for all,"
one of the brothers said.

The brothers took Joseph's coat, then they **threw** him down a dry well.

"Help!"

They sold him as a **slave** to passing traders going to Egypt.

The brothers told Jacob that Joseph had been **killed** by a wild animal.

33

Joseph was bought by an Egyptian called Potiphar.

He was captain of the soldiers who guarded Pharaoh, the king of Egypt.

With God's help, Joseph did his duties well.

34

But one day, Potiphar's wife tricked Joseph, and he was thrown into prison.

35

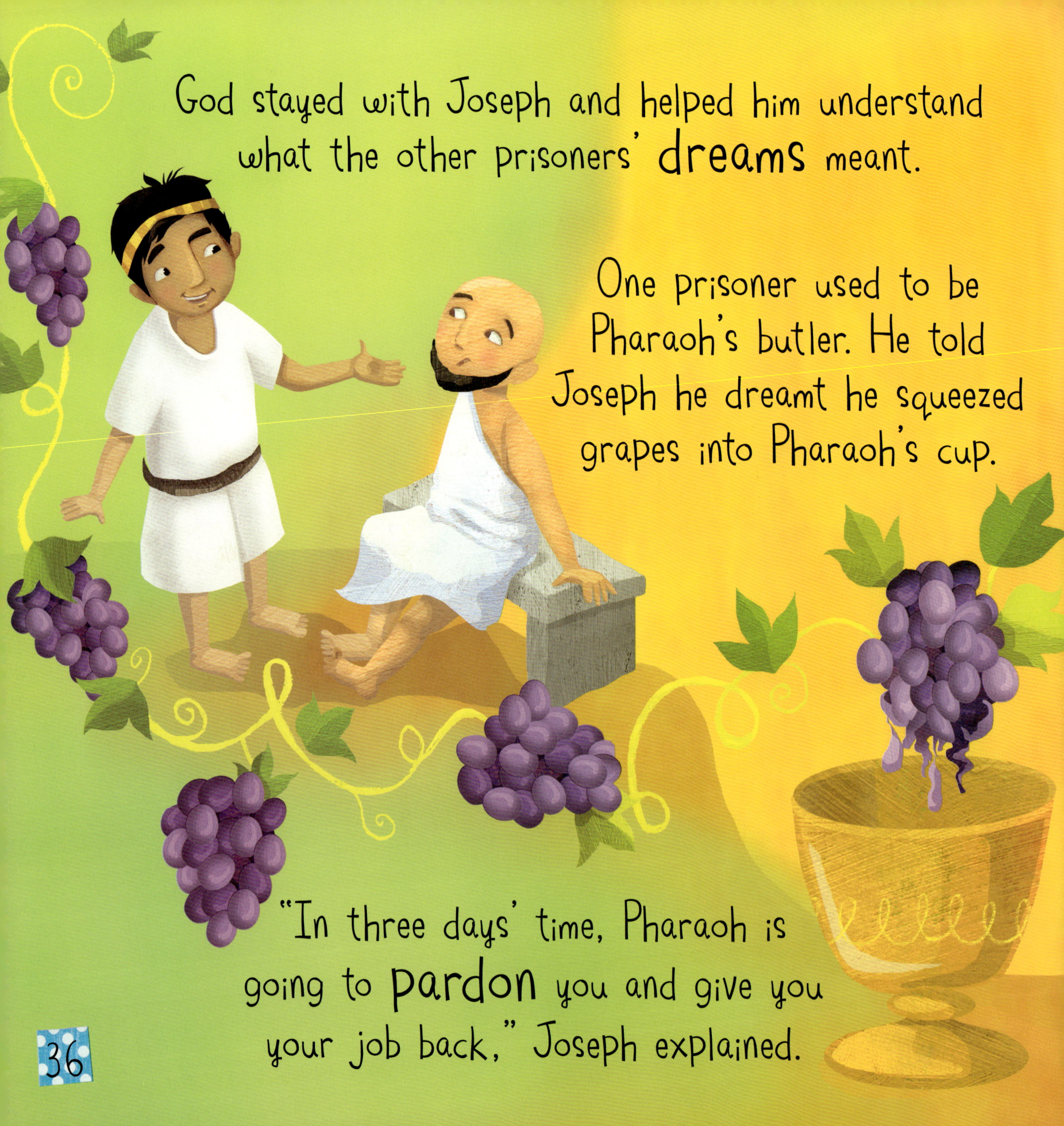

God stayed with Joseph and helped him understand what the other prisoners' **dreams** meant.

One prisoner used to be Pharaoh's butler. He told Joseph he dreamt he squeezed grapes into Pharaoh's cup.

"In three days' time, Pharaoh is going to **pardon** you and give you your job back," Joseph explained.

Another prisoner told Joseph, "I dreamt I was carrying three baskets of bread, but birds were eating it."

Joseph's face fell, and he said sadly, "In three days' time, you will die."

The dreams came true.

37

One morning, Pharaoh awoke after two strange dreams.

In the first dream, seven fat COWS were eaten by seven thin cows!

In the second dream, seven small, shrivelled ears of **corn** swallowed up seven big, full ears of corn.

Pharaoh's butler remembered Joseph, so Pharaoh sent for him at once.

Pharaoh described his dreams to Joseph, and God told him what they meant.

"For the next seven years, Egypt will have good harvests," Joseph said. "But during the seven years after, the crops will fail and there won't be enough food."

Pharaoh was so pleased with Joseph that he put him in **charge** of Egypt.

For seven years, Joseph **stored** plenty of food.

Then the crops failed, and the bad harvests began.

People came from far and wide to ask for **food**.

One day, Joseph's brothers came, but they didn't recognize Joseph after all this time.

'I need to make sure they have **changed**,' Joseph thought to himself.

When the brothers were heading home, loaded with food, they were stopped by Joseph's guards.

The guards found Joseph's best silver cup in one of their sacks. Joseph had **hidden** it there as a trick.

The brothers were taken to Joseph, who said, "Benjamin must stay here. The rest of you are **free** to go."

46

"Our father has already lost his **favourite** son. Let us stay instead of him," the brothers pleaded.

Then Joseph told his brothers who he really was. They were **shocked** when they found out. 47

Joseph **forgave** his brothers and was reunited with his father, Jacob.

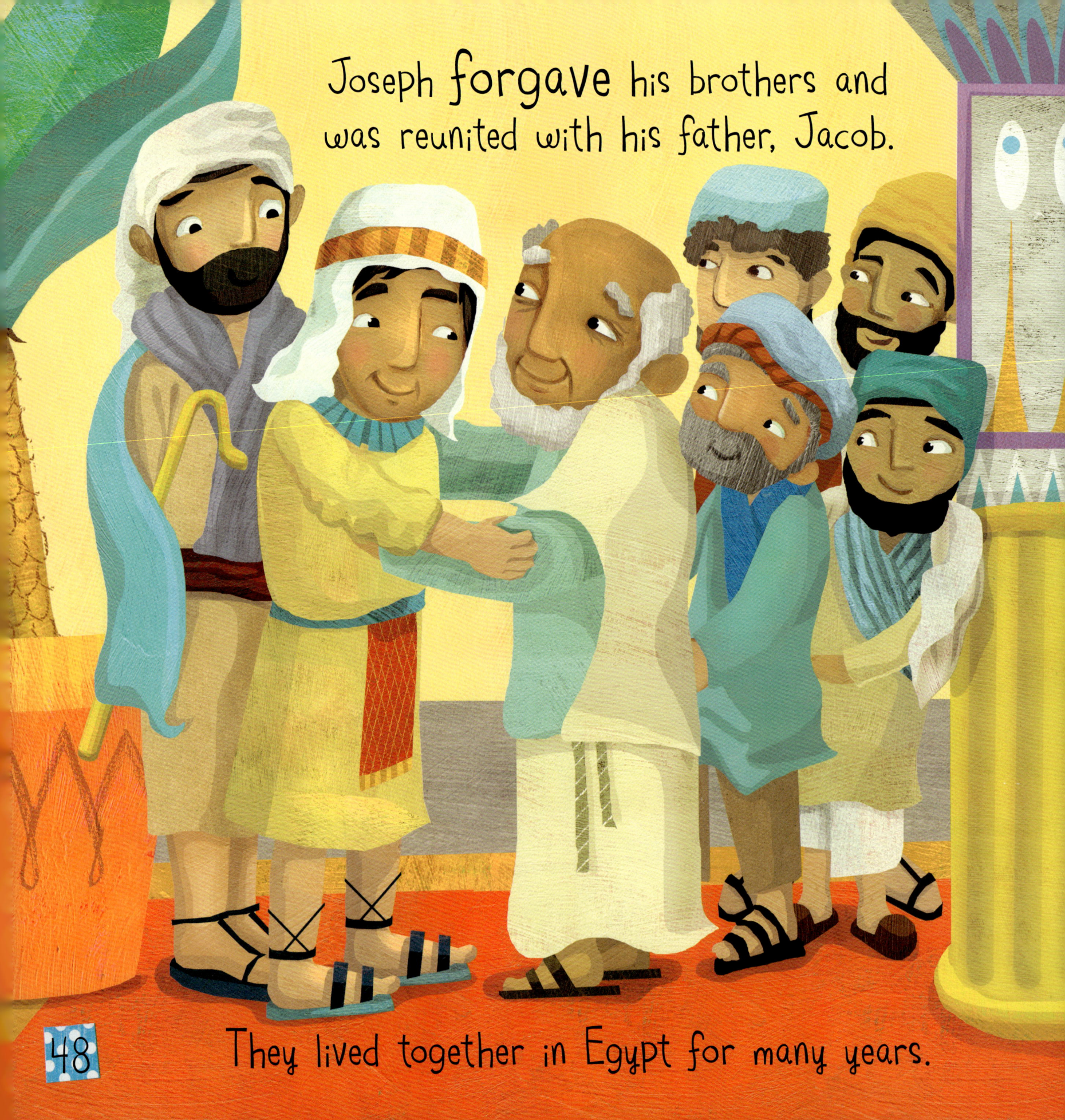

They lived together in Egypt for many years.

Moses in the Bulrushes

Long ago in Egypt there lived a group of people called the Israelites.

They lived **peacefully** among the Egyptian people, where some became rich.

51

After many years, there were a lot of Israelite people living in Egypt.

The king of Egypt, or Pharaoh, wasn't happy that there were so many Israelites in his country.

He thought that one day they would try to **take over Egypt.**

Pharaoh forced the Israelites to become slaves. They had to work for the Egyptian people to build new towns, and were treated harshly.

But the number of Israelite people **continued to grow.**

Pharaoh needed another plan to stop the Israelites becoming powerful.

Pharaoh ordered that all Israelite baby boys were killed, but that girls were allowed to live.

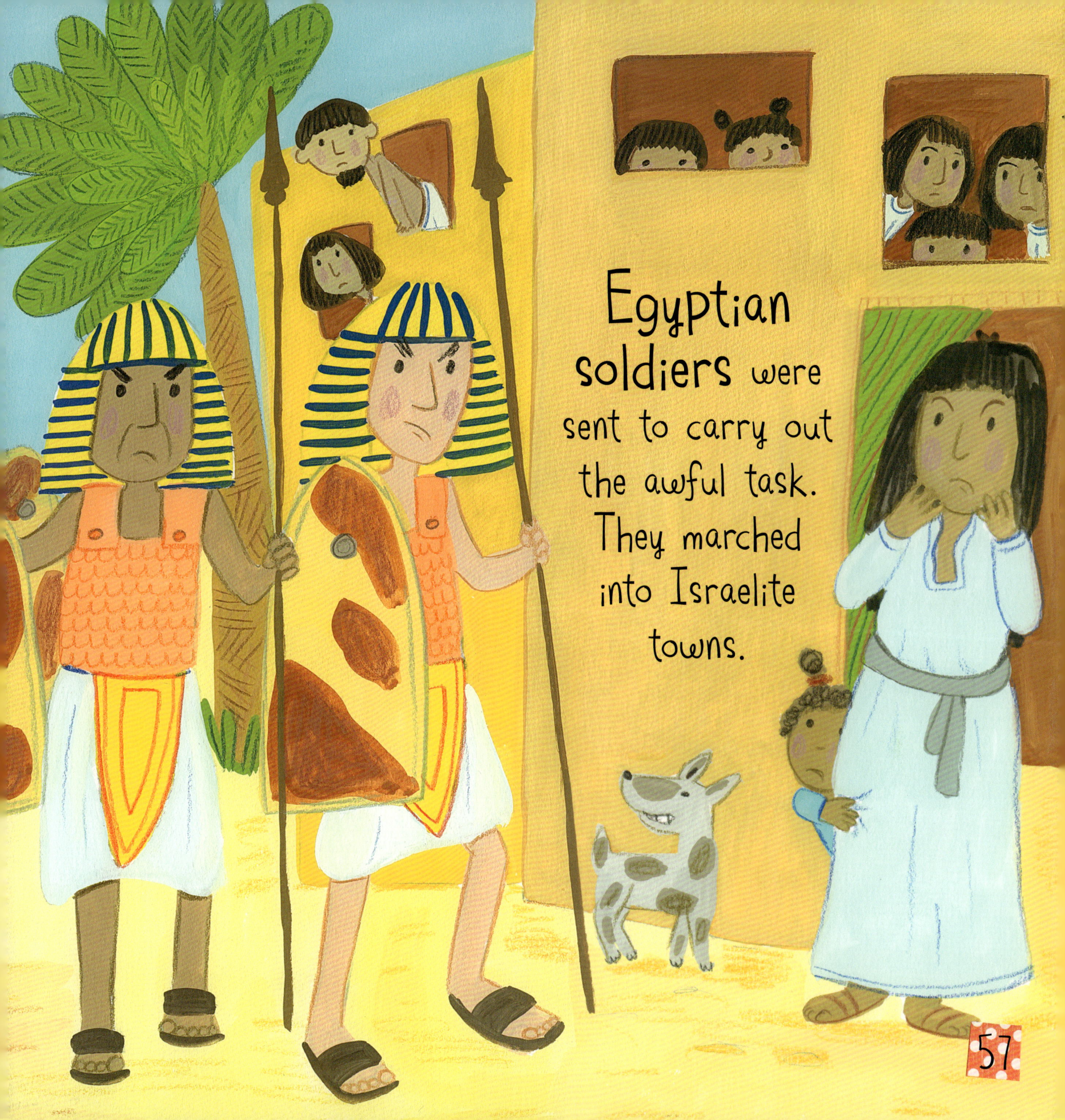

Egyptian soldiers were sent to carry out the awful task. They marched into Israelite towns.

57

One Israelite family had a **tiny baby boy.** They managed to hide him from the Pharaoh's soldiers.

Sshh!

For three months they were able to keep the baby boy a secret.

Waah!

But as he began to grow **bigger and noisier,** this became more difficult.

59

One day, the baby's mother came up with a plan. She made a **strong basket** and coated it with tar to make it waterproof.

The baby's sister, Miriam, watched closely.

Then they wrapped
the baby in a blanket
to keep him warm, and
put him in the basket.

Then Miriam and her mother crept down to the river and placed the basket with the sleeping baby among the **tall bulrushes.**

The little basket bobbed gently on the water.

Miriam's mother returned home
to stop people becoming suspicious.
Miriam hid in the bulrushes and
kept watch over her baby brother.

After a while, Miriam saw some people approaching — it was Pharaoh's daughter and her servants!

The princess had come to the **river** to bathe.

Suddenly the princess noticed the little basket floating gently on the water.

"Quickly! Fetch that basket!" she ordered one of her servants.

65

The servant pulled the basket from the water and gasped when she saw the little baby boy inside. He began to cry.

"Give the child to me," said the princess, and she held him in her arms.

Suddenly, Miriam appeared before the princess. "Perhaps I could find someone to help look after the baby?"

"Yes," said the princess. "Find me a nurse."

Miriam hurried to bring her mother to the princess.

"I will pay you to look after this child, he will be brought up as my son and no harm will come to him."

68

Miriam and her mother were **overjoyed**.

The princess named the baby 'Moses', which means 'drawn out', just as he was drawn out of the water.

So, as a small child, Moses stayed with his family, living **safely and happily** under the protection of the princess.

Then one day when he was old
enough, his mother and sister
took him to the Pharaoh's
palace to be with the princess.

71

"Thank you for looking after him," said the princess. So, Moses was brought up as an Egyptian prince.

Little did he know that one day he would help to set the Israelite people free, under God's guidance.

David and Goliath

Thousands of years ago, in a land called Judea, there lived an Israelite boy called David. He was the youngest of eight brothers.

He spent his days working as a shepherd boy. Even though he was young, David was **brave**. He often fought off bears from his flock.

One day, David's father asked him to take some food to his brothers, who were away fighting for the Israelite army.

A group of people called the Philistines were trying to invade their land, and the battle was fierce.

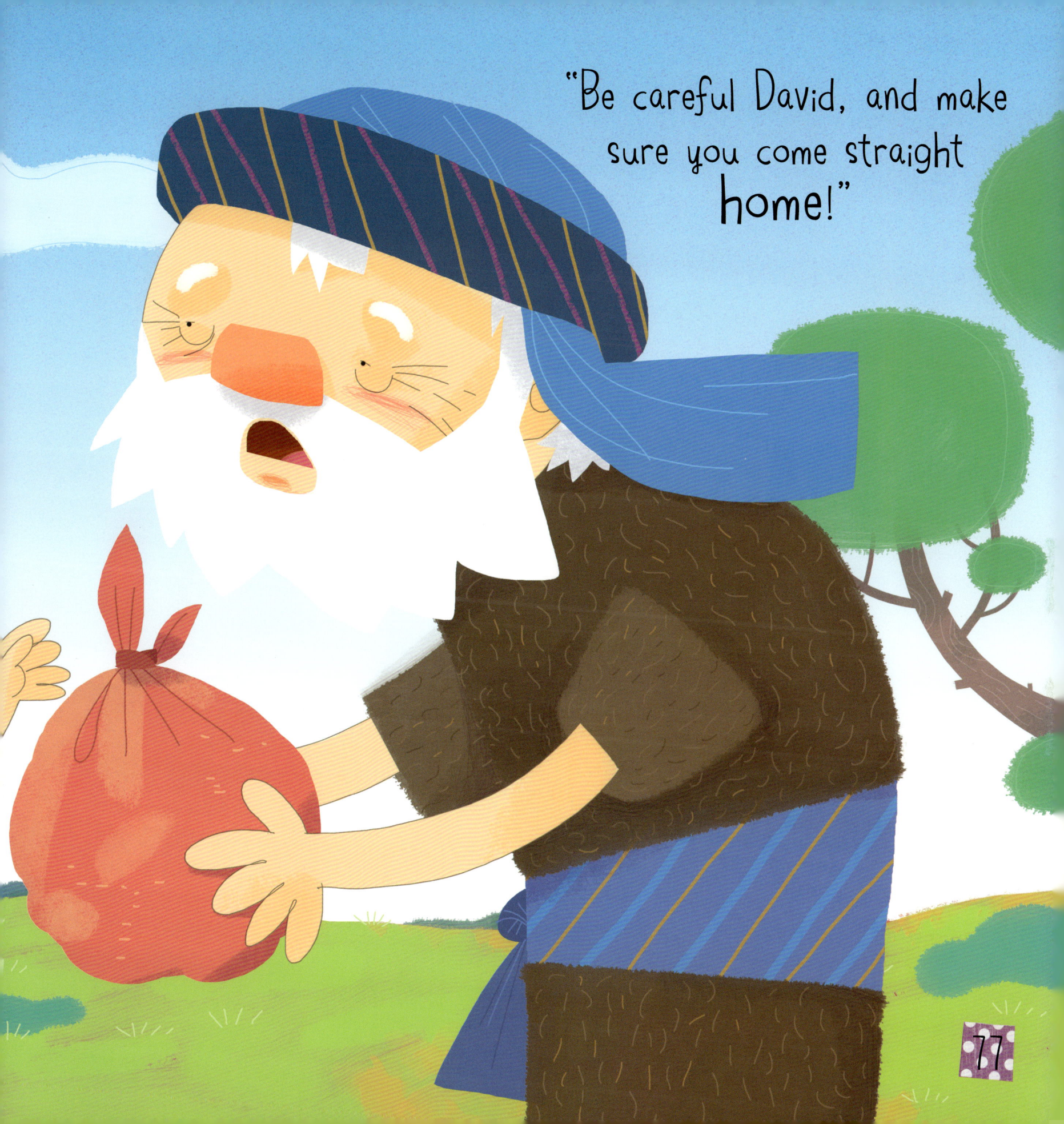

"Be careful David, and make sure you come straight **home!**"

When David arrived at the
army camp, he found all
the soldiers in a panic.

He searched for his brothers and asked them what was happening. "The enemy have a **giant** with them!" they cried.

"Run away if you like," the giant bellowed. "Instead of a huge battle, send someone to fight me in single combat. Whoever wins has victory for their side!"

81

The giant smashed his mighty spear against his shield and threw back his head and **roared**, and the noise crashed around the surrounding hills like thunder.

The soldiers huddled together, unsure what to do. No one felt brave enough to take on the giant by themselves.

David, who was still stood in the camp, was outraged. "I will fight the giant!" he shouted.

"Let me at him!"

Nothing anyone could say could persuade David otherwise. He was determined to fight.

At last the king agreed David could
fight the giant but he insisted on
dressing David in his own armour.

But when David put it on, it
was so big and bulky that
he couldn't move.

David walked down to a nearby stream and picked up five smooth **stones**, placing them in his shepherd's pouch.

Then he strode out to meet the giant, whose name was Goliath of Gath.

He only had his slingshot and the stones.

The giant burst out **laughing** at the sight of the young boy, but David stood there calmly. He knew he had God on his side.

"What is this, a young boy dares to challenge me!" the giant laughed.

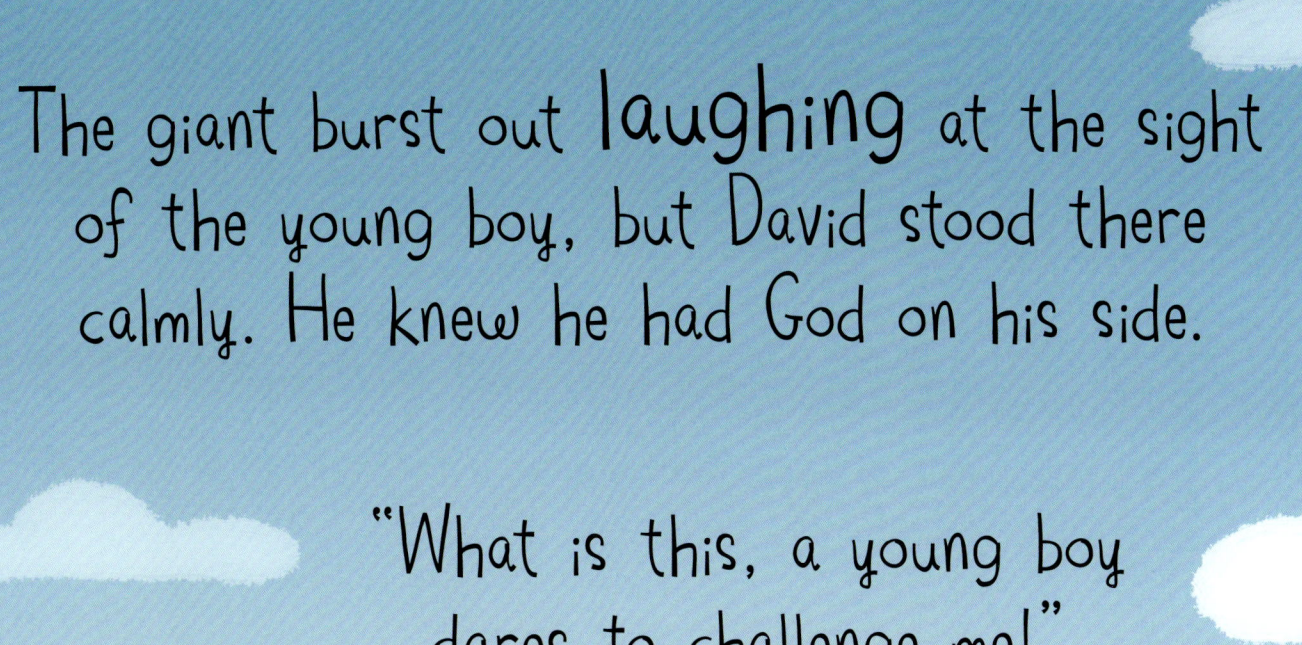

The king and his army watched as the giant ran towards David, brandishing his spear.

David darted and dashed around the giant's feet.

The giant couldn't catch him!

93

Then David raised his slingshot and whirled it around...
A stone struck Goliath in the forehead, sending
him crashing to the ground, **dead**.

Everyone jumped up
cheering, the giant
had been **defeated!**

95

The Philistine army turned and fled. The Israelites had won the battle at last!

"David is our hero!"

96